NANA NEEDS A RUTABAGA
Noah and Ethan Save the Day

Written by *Sherry Karuza Waldrip*

Illustrated by *Eric Walls*

Colby~

Watch out for the monkeys!

♡ Miss Sherry

Dedicated to:

MY wonderful Nana, Gladys

Thank you for loving and delighting in a zany little girl many years ago

"I love you a bushel and a peck and a hug around the neck"

I think of you and miss you every single day!

And

Our superheroes, Noah and Ethan

Our delightful granddaughters, Kyra and Danyella

Nana Needs a Rutabaga
© 2014 by Sherry Karuza Waldrip

Illustrations by Eric Walls
www.ericwallsillustration.com

Author photo by Carrie Allen Photography

Printed in the USA by

www.crownmediacorp.com

ISBN 978-0-692-25876-7

My name is Noah and I'm four, almost five. My brother, Ethan, is three, almost four. One day, we were wrestling with Papa and Nana said,

"Let's go to Barney's Sooper Market. Nana needs a rutabaga for the stew."

I didn't know what a rutabaga was, but I'm sure it isn't as good as pizza!

"Why can't we just have pizza?" I pleaded.

Nana said, "Because little taste buds need to experience variety." Whatever that is!

"Will Barney be there?" I inquired.

"Barney who?" Nana asked.

"Barney from the sooper market!" I replied.

Nana said, "I don't think so, sweetheart."

"Then, we want to stay here with Papa!" I said firmly.

Nana said if we went with her, we could pick out the ice cream. So we jumped up real fast. My brother and I LOVE ice cream!

I don't know why they don't have a picture of Barney on the front of the store. Everyone would go there if they did! Ethan and I always look around the corners and past the green beans real fast, but we have never seen him. A big purple dinosaur should be pretty easy to spot. He must come in on Tuesdays, instead.

Nana picked the car cart with two steering wheels so my brother and I could both steer. We tried real hard to steer good so Nana didn't run into stuff. When we steered Nana down the cookie aisle, Ethan and I heard the weirdest noise! It sounded kind of like screeching. We looked and looked to see if it was Barney. We glanced up at Nana, but she was reading something on a cereal box. We heard it again! We looked at each other, and then we looked on the shelf, you know, the second shelf from the bottom. Wow! Look at that! It was coming from that box, that box of Animal Crackers!

I said, "Ethan! Go get that box and don't let Nana see you!" When you have a little brother, lots of times you can get him to do stuff you want, and you are not the one who gets into trouble.

Nana was still reading the box when Ethan jumped back into the cart with the Animal Crackers. The box shook and wiggled and jumped right out of his hands. I caught it just in the nick of time.

Ethan watched as I took my finger and very carefully pulled up the top of the box. My brother and I almost fell right out of the cart and onto the floor when a monkey climbed out of the box and looked right straight at us. He tilted and then scratched his head like WE were the ones who were strange! Can you imagine that? Gee Whiz, monkeys are gobs more out of the ordinary at a sooper market than boys are!

The monkey leaped off the cart and scooted down the aisle. Boy, oh Boy, we were going to get in SO much trouble. I think there must be a rule about letting a monkey run crazy in a grocery store, even if the store is owned by a really cool dinosaur named Barney. You know grownups. They have rules about everything! We looked up at our Nana, and she was talking to a lady with funny hair and didn't even seem to notice that a wild monkey was about to go on a rampage!

My brother and I looked at each other. I told him, "We got trouble!" Ethan said, "Big! Huge!" That's what he always says when there is big trouble. Without saying another word, we knew it was up to us to save the day.

We jumped out of the cart and ran over to the vegetable aisle to grab a can of spinach. We knew we needed big muscles like Popeye if we were going to wrestle with a monkey. After all, we were only almost four and almost five. I tried with all my might to squeeze that can of spinach just like Popeye does, but it wouldn't even budge. So Ethan snatched it from my grip. In a brilliant maneuver, my brother jumped on the can, and the spinach busted out on the floor. If Nana knew we were about to eat off the floor she would have a conniption fit, even if it was a vegetable! Nana worries a lot about germs.

We grabbed a handful of spinach and shoved it into our mouths. Eeeeewwww! This stuff's nasty! Popeye must eat a different brand or something!

In my best and deepest big boy voice, I hollered, "Cleanup on aisle two!" Then we scurried around the corner. We were on a mission and couldn't risk being nabbed by Mr. John for making a mess.

We hustled over to the toy aisle and found a super soaker!

We skedaddled back over to Mr. T's meat department and snatched the net off the wall from the seafood display. Then we ran over to aisle eleven, the hardware aisle, to get some rope. Next, we were off to pick up some snacks. No, silly, not for us; we needed bait! Everyone knows that monkey's love peanuts.

Holy Smoke! Ethan was moving through the aisles as fast as Robin and, of course, I would be Batman because I'm bigger…I'm almost five!

We skidded around the corner. There he was, very close to the rutabagas, just as happy as he could be, sitting right smack in the middle of the bananas. He was using very bad manners as he shoved bananas in his mouth and threw the peels on the floor. What a terrible mess!

Jeepers! We had to act fast or we were going to have grownups sliding all over Mr. Steve's produce department on banana peels! We had to stop and giggle for a second because that would look pretty funny for sure!

Nana was still talking to the lady over by the peanut butter. That's good, because she would never let us do what we had to do.

I threw the rope over the light and climbed up to the ceiling while Ethan distracted the monkey with the super soaker, so I could shimmy down the rope and drop the net.

Boy, oh Boy, was that naughty monkey ever surprised! He jumped up and down and squealed like nobody's business. To calm him down, Ethan gave him the peanuts. It worked! He just sat right down in the middle of the bananas grinning like a silly monkey and popped peanuts down, one right after another. You can get a monkey to do almost anything with the proper snacks.

We took a deep breath and shoved with all our might until the monkey popped back into the Animal Cracker box. Then, we ran back over to aisle eleven to get some tape and secured the box.

We put the box back on aisle six, second shelf from the bottom. We made a b-line back to Nana's cart. We climbed back behind the steering wheels just as Nana said goodbye to her lady friend.

Whew! I didn't want to admit it, but saving the day was very hard work. I knew we were going to need a nap when we went back to Nana and Papa's house.

Nana looked down at us and said, "My goodness, you boys have been so well behaved. I think we should buy some Animal Crackers to go with our ice cream tonight."

Ethan and I both shouted, "NO! We don't think Animal Crackers would taste very good tonight!"

Nana looked surprised and said, "Alright, that's okay, boys; just choose something else." You should have seen the look on Nana's face when we pointed at the Fig Newton's! We sure didn't want Animal Crackers, and that's a fact!

We hurried real fast and drove our Nana's cart right straight over to Miss Terry's check-out and parked right behind the lady with funny hair.

When we were leaving, I heard a funny noise. I peeked over my shoulder and could see the animal cracker box begin to wobble again. I grabbed my brother and said, "Yikes! Come on Ethan. Let's get out of here!" and we scurried after our Nana.

When we got home, Papa asked us how things went at Barneys. Nana said, "The boys were certainly on their best behavior. But, you know Papa, grocery shopping is pretty uneventful."

Ethan and I rolled our eyes and laughed until our tummy's hurt. We found shopping for a rutabaga to be quite an adventure. Maybe, next time, Nana will take us on a Tuesday, and Barney will be there.

Sherry Waldrip spent many years as a domestic goddess taking care of her family of men. Cleaning toilets was her life. In 1991, she was diagnosed with breast cancer and later wrote the humorous and inspirational book, *I Don't Remember Signing up for Cancer!* Her book was the recipient of an *Excellence in Media International Angel Award.* She is a national speaker and humorist for survivor celebrations and events.

When her grandsons arrived on the scene, just a year and two weeks apart, she regularly snuggled them on her lap and made up silly stories off the top of her head. Noah and Ethan were always the protagonists who were off on a fantasy adventure. Her little men loved these stories, but their reaction to this one went off the giggle-meter. The following day, she decided to write it down, and it became her first children's book, *Nana Needs a Rutabaga.*

www.sherrywaldrip.com

Illustrator **Eric Walls** has spent over twenty years as a character animator for numerous family feature films, including *Beauty and the Beast, The Lion King, The Prince of Egypt, Meet the Robinsons, Bolt,* and *The Princess and the Frog.* As an illustrator, Eric uses his vast experience to help independent authors and publishers realize their dream of bringing their children's picture book to reality.

You can learn more about Eric's illustration services at:

www.ericwallsillustration.com

Thank you to:

Jean Wilde

My editor, my sister-in-law and the first one to insist this story was
worthy of publication

***

Jody Bernard

My friend, an elementary school teacher, who fell in love with my story, set up
readings to test the kids' reactions, introduced me to teachers and librarians
and became my unending cheerleader

***

Jerry Waldrip

My husband, for being my love and my superhero

***

Michael Waldrip

Our firstborn, for his love, encouragement and marketing advice

***

David Waldrip

Our youngest, for his love, humor and for making me a Nana

***

Erika Waldrip

Our daughter-in-law, for joining our family and bringing us our
fabulous granddaughters

***

Eric Walls

For creating the perfect illustrations to bring my story to life

***

My amazing focus group kids at my favorite elementary school

For loving my story and being such an cncouragement

***

And all those who encouraged me along the way